Stories and rhymes in this book

THE WIGGLY WORMS
WILMA GOES STRAIGHT
WHETHER THE SOIL...
CREEPY CRAWLIES UNITED
MUNCHERS BEWARE!
UNDER THE FLOWER BED AND FAR AWAY
UNDERNEATH THE FLOWER BED
WILMA AND THE APPLE
I CAN...

Published by Ladybird Books Ltd
27 Wrights Lane London W8 5TZ
A Penguin Company
5 7 9 10 8 6 4

© LADYBIRD BOOKS LTD MCMXCIX

Produced for Ladybird Books Ltd by Nicola Baxter and Amanda Hawkes
The moral rights of the autor/illustrator have been asserted
LADYBIRD and the device of a Ladybird are trademarks of Ladybird Books Ltd

Printed in Italy

The Wiggly Worms

by Mandy Ross

illustrated by Caroline Jayne Church

Ladybird

THE WIGGLY WORMS

In a wiggly house
with wiggly floors,

And wiggly
windows,

And wiggly
doors,

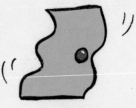

Live the Wiggly, Wriggly,
Squiggly Worms!

They have wiggly beds, And wiggly chairs,

And wiggly carpets,
Up wiggly stairs,

Have the Wiggly, Wriggly, Squiggly Worms!

WILMA GOES STRAIGHT

The Wiggly Worm family
lived in a wiggly house
under the flower bed,
where nothing was
quite straight.

There was William Worm...

and Wilma Worm...

and their mum,
Mrs Wendy Worm...

and
Grandpa Wilby Worm.

One day,
Wilma Worm
decided to
measure
herself.

First she untied a knot at
the end of her tail.

Then she lay down next to the Length Chart on the wiggly wall.

"I'm sure I'd be longer if I was straight," said Wilma.

So she stretched and...

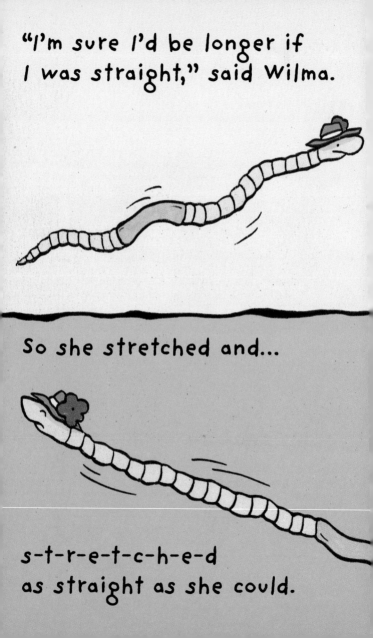

s-t-r-e-t-c-h-e-d
as straight as she could.

And she
was right!
She was
m-u-c-h
l-o-n-g-e-r.

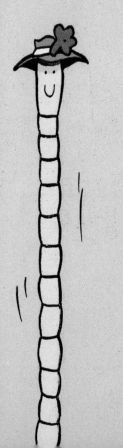

"Bedtime!"
called Mum
just then.
"Straight to
bed, please."

So Wilma
did as she
was told.

She went straight to bed...

and she found she was
MUCH too long.

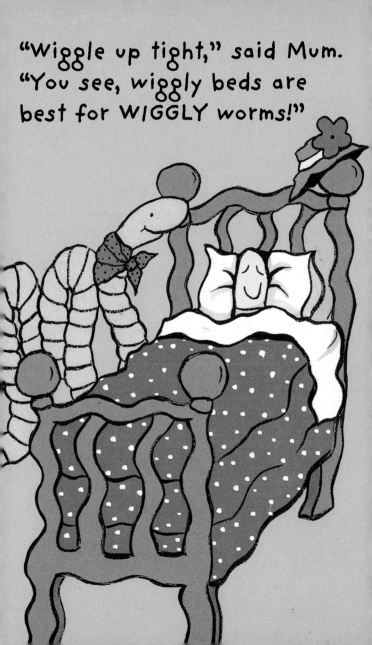

WHETHER THE SOIL...

Whether the soil is wet and squelchy,

Whether the soil is firm,

Whether the soil is warm and crumbly,

It's wonderful being a worm!

CREEPY CRAWLIES UNITED

The creepy crawlies' football team were tying their bootlaces ready for the match.

Lydia Ladybird had six bows to tie.

Stephen Spider had eight.

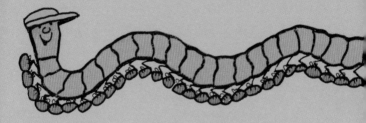

Celia Centipede had
almost a hundred.

Captain Millie Millipede
couldn't even count how
many bows she had to tie.
It took ages!

"Can we play?" asked Wilma and William Worm.

"Sorry," sniffed Stephen Spider. "You've got no football boots."

"And you've got no LEGS!"
shouted Celia Centipede.

And she waved so many of
her legs that she fell over.

"Just you watch," said the Wiggly Worms. And they called over their friends, Simon Snail and Sue Slug.

William, Wilma, Simon and Sue wiggled and...

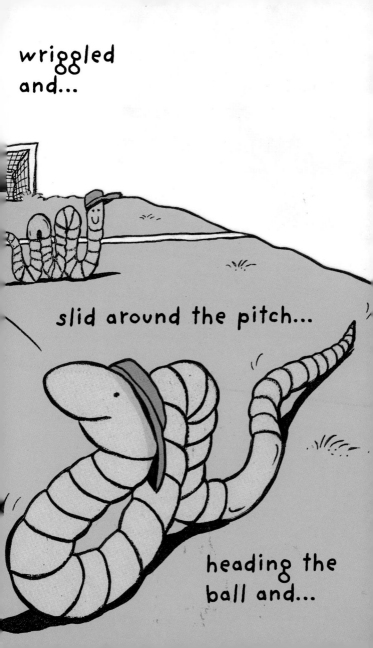

making fantastic slithering saves.

They left the other creepy crawlies standing!

Captain
Millie
Millipede
blew her
whistle.

"That's wigglingly
brilliant!" she shouted.

"Come and join our team!"

MUNCHERS BEWARE!

I love to munch an apple,

I love to munch a pear,

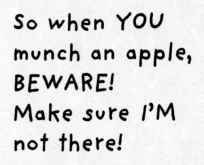

So when YOU munch an apple, BEWARE! Make sure I'M not there!

UNDER THE FLOWER BED AND FAR AWAY

"Today I'm going to dig the longest, wiggliest tunnel in the world," said William Worm,

"under the flower bed and far away!"

Wilma and Mum
and Grandpa Wilby
wiggled along
behind...

to find out
where
William was
going.

Every so often, they met
another creepy crawly.

"Hello, Millie Millipede!" called William as he wiggled past.

And then... "Hello, Celia Centipede!"

And then... "Hello! Who's that ahead?"

William tried to catch up
with the creepy crawly
ahead.

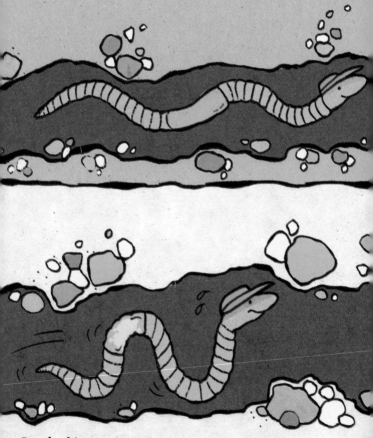

But the faster he wiggled...

the faster it went, too.
"Stop!" called William.

At last, William Worm
caught up with the creepy
crawly and grabbed its tail.

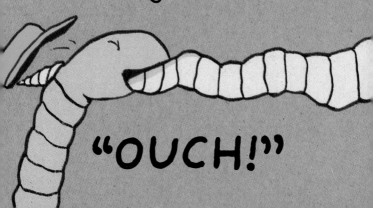

"OUCH!"

shouted
Grandpa
Wilby!

"Grandpa Wilby!" cried William. "What are you doing in front of me?"

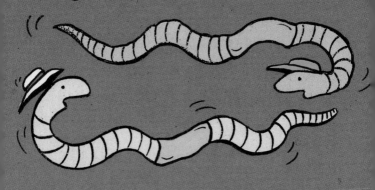

"William!" cried Grandpa Wilby. "What are you doing behind me?"

"I know!" said Wilma. "William's dug such a long and wiggly tunnel that...

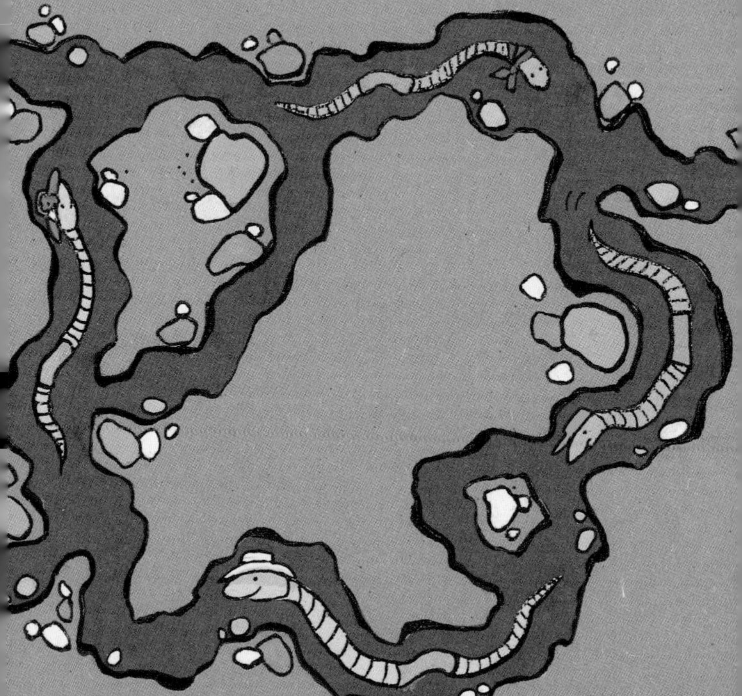

he's gone right round in a squiggly circle!"

UNDERNEATH THE FLOWER BED

Underneath the flower bed,
I'm happy when I wiggle.

The flower roots are tickly,
And they always make
me giggle!

WILMA AND THE APPLE

Wilma Worm
loved to eat
ripe, rosy
red apples.
Every day
she waited
under the
apple tree
for an apple
to fall...

KERPLONK!

Then she would munch...

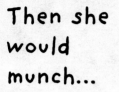

and crunch...

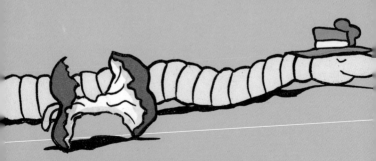

till she was as full as a worm could be.

One day,
Wilma
waited...

and
waited...

but no apples fell.
So she decided
to climb the tree.

At last she reached a ripe, rosy red apple.

She munched and crunched till she was as full as a worm could be...

and she fell asleep, right there inside the apple.

Suddenly, there was a
WHIZZZ... KERPLONK!

Inside the apple, Wilma woke with a start. "Where am I?" she gasped.

And then she heard a loud
MUNCH... CR-R-RUNCH.
"What's that?" she cried.

"Wilma!" said William.
"I've found you! Right inside
my snack!"

Wilma wiggled out of the apple.

"From now on, I'll wait for apples to fall before I eat them!" she said.

I CAN...

"I can fly,"
said the fly,
As it flew
in the sky.

"I can swim,"
said the fish,
As it swam
with a swish.

"I can leap,"
said the frog,
As it leapt
off a log.

But no one
can squirm
As well as
a worm!

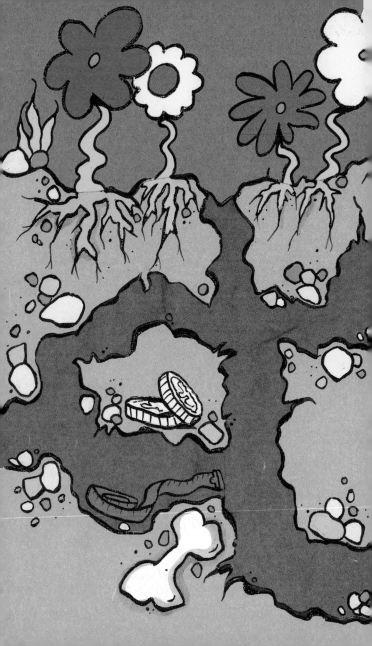